The Arabic Quilt

An Immigrant Story

Written by
Aya Khalil

Illustrated by
Anait Semirdzhyan

TILBURY HOUSE PUBLISHERS, THOMASTON, MAINE

Text © 2020 by Aya Khalil
Illustrations © 2020 by Anait Semirdzhayan

Hardcover ISBN 978-0-88448-754-8 · First hardcover printing January 2020

Tilbury House Publishers · 12 Starr Street · Thomaston, Maine 04861 · www.tilburyhouse.com

Library of Congress
Control Number: 2019954510

Designed by Frame25 Productions
Printed in Korea

15 16 17 18 19 20 XXX 10 9 8 7

To Tota and Geddo. —A.K.

To my bilingual twins, Yulia and Yana. —A.S.

"Kanzi, *habibti*, you're going to be late to the first day of school," Mama calls.

"I'm coming, Mama." Kanzi stuffs her notebook into her backpack and quickly but carefully folds her quilt—the special one Teita made in Egypt.

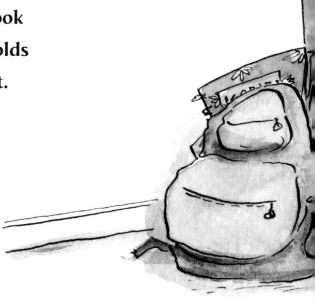

Breakfast is delicious: Egyptian fava beans, homemade French toast, and watermelon with feta cheese and mint. Zacharia has watermelon juice dripping down his chin. He looks happy.

"I packed your favorite lunch for you: a *kofta* sandwich!" Baba exclaims.

"*Shukran*, Baba," Kanzi says, but secretly she wishes her baba would pack her a peanut butter and jelly sandwich instead. Her family has just moved to this town, and she doesn't know anyone. She doesn't want to be different.

In the car, Mama sings along with the songs on the Arabic radio channel. When they pull up to the school, Kanzi turns down the radio volume. Mama gives her a confused look.

"Good luck today," Mama says. "*Bahebek*."

"I love you, too," Kanzi responds.

In class, Mrs. Haugen asks all the students to share three facts about themselves.

When it is Kanzi's turn, she says bravely, "I am Egyptian-American. I love to swim. I love to write poetry!" Then she sits, looking down at her desk.

At lunchtime, Kanzi is surprised when Mama walks through the door. "*Habibti*, you forgot your lunchbox!"

"*Habibti*? Like *The Hobbit*? Isn't your name Kanzi?" Molly snickers. Her classmates laugh with her as they walk to the cafeteria.

Mrs. Haugen sees tears rolling down Kanzi's cheeks. "What's wrong?" she asks.

"Molly made fun of what my mama said," Kanzi replies.

"Oh, Kanzi, being bilingual is beautiful," says Mrs. Haugen. "Don't let anyone make you feel ashamed. You are special."

That night, as Mama puts leftover
shurbet 'ads in Kanzi's lunchbox, Kanzi gently pats
Mama's back. "Can you please pack me a turkey sandwich instead?"

Before bed, Kanzi writes a poem as she hugs her quilt, which smells like Teita's home.

The next day Molly says, "Mrs. Haugen said
I hurt your feelings. I'm sorry I laughed at
your mom's language. It sounded funny."

"It may sound funny to you, but that is only because you don't speak Arabic," Kanzi says. She feels a lump forming in her throat. "My parents say that learning different languages makes a person smarter and kinder," she blurts out.

"OK, whatever," Molly says, skipping away.

Mrs. Haugen calls Kanzi to her desk after lunch. "I found this notebook on the floor, and it was opened to a lovely poem," she says.

"I was describing my teita's quilt," Kanzi says. "When I visited her in Egypt, she gave it to me. My teita only speaks Arabic."

Mrs. Haugen smiles. "That is special. I would love to see your quilt."

"Can I bring it to school?" Kanzi asks.

"Sure, bring it tomorrow," Mrs. Haugen says.

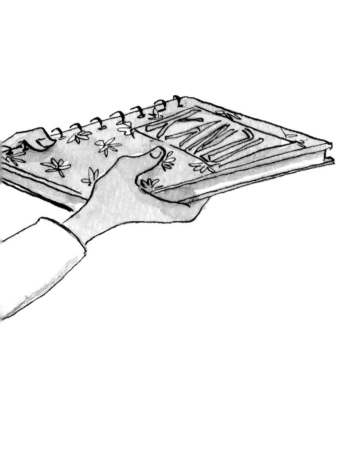

The next day Kanzi unfolds her quilt in front of the class. Her heart is pounding. "This is my quilt that my teita in Egypt made," she says.

"That's cool! I want to make a quilt like that!" DeShawn says.

"Maybe we can all make one for our classroom!" Claire shouts.

Mrs. Haugen nods and smiles.

On Friday, Mrs. Haugen makes an announcement. "I have an exciting project for us all to work on. Kanzi's mom is here to help us make a quilt of all your names in Arabic."

As Mama steps forward,
Kanzi thinks how beautiful she looks.
"*Shukran* for welcoming me here!" Mama says.
"Kanzi and I will write down your names in
Arabic, and you will copy your name on your own quilt piece."

Molly is not enthusiastic about the project. "Who cares about Arabic? We live in America. My mom says we should only speak English."

In response, Mrs. Haugen starts writing words on the board: algebra, coffee, lemon, sugar.

"Does anyone know what these words have in common?" she asks.

"They come from Arabic words," Kanzi whispers.

Mrs. Haugen nods. "Learning other languages besides the one we grow up with helps make the world a friendlier place. We can speak non-English languages and still be American."

"I wonder what *my* name looks like in Arabic," Brianna says.

Kanzi and Mama write down everyone's names.

"Neat! *Shukran*!" Aminah exclaims.

Everyone copies their Arabic names onto sheets of colored paper. Then they decorate their papers with glitter and jewels and place them on the table for the glue to dry. "On Monday morning you will see a beautiful class quilt hanging in the hall," Mrs. Haugen tells them.

Kanzi is nervous when the bell rings on
Monday morning and the kids file into school.
What if the quilt didn't turn out nicely?

The quilt hangs on the bulletin board outside Mrs. Haugen's classroom. The colorful papers with their Arabic names have been cut into different shapes and sizes, and all the pieces are stapled together. Kanzi stands in awe, reading names in Arabic: Claire, Leah, Molly, Ivy, Jack, Lucas, Brianna, Chang, DeShawn, Sam, Angela, Lily, Aminah. Teachers and older students stop to look at the names, trying to figure out whose name is whose. "Wow, look at those beautiful letters—they're like drawings!" they say.

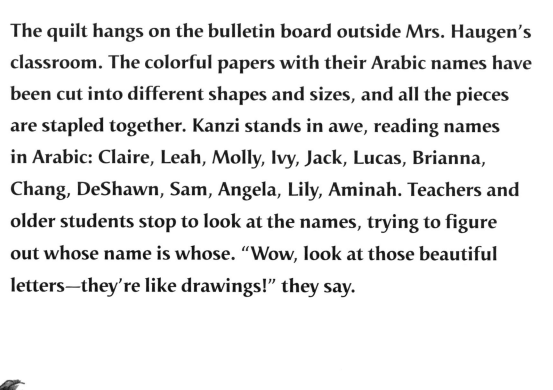

"That was a really cool project, Kanzi. *Shukran*," Kanzi's classmates tell her.

"I'm sorry I made fun of you," says Molly. "I didn't realize how important a different language is. Can you write my mom's name in Arabic? I want to give it to her as a gift."

"Okay,"
Kanzi says.

"Do you want to go swimming soon?"

"I'd love to," Kanzi nods, as Molly hugs her.

Leaving class a week later, Kanzi stops to look at the Arabic quilt one last time.

Right across from it she is surprised to see another collage of names in a language she doesn't recognize. "Those are my classmates' names in Japanese!" Kura says. "Our teacher was inspired by your classroom's idea, and she asked me to help write everyone's name in Japanese. Aren't languages a beautiful thing? They can truly unite us!"

Kanzi smiles in agreement.

In her room that night, Kanzi holds Teita's quilt
tightly as she writes a poem for her parents.

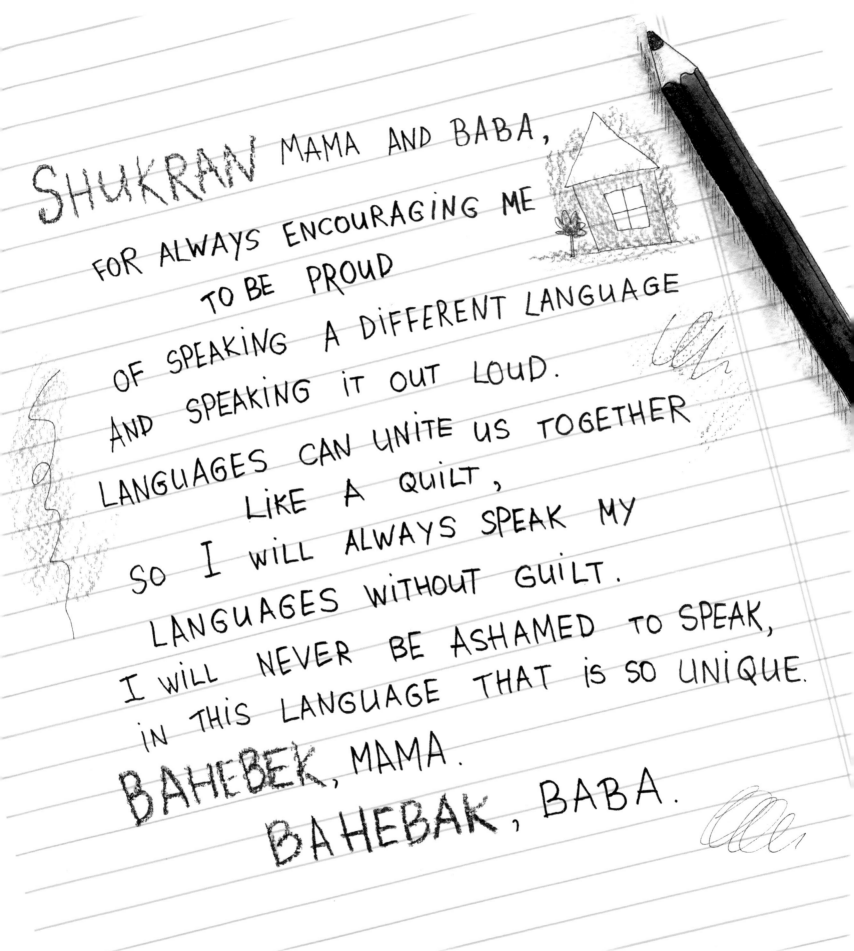

SHUKRAN MAMA AND BABA,
FOR ALWAYS ENCOURAGING ME
TO BE PROUD
OF SPEAKING A DIFFERENT LANGUAGE
AND SPEAKING IT OUT LOUD.
LANGUAGES CAN UNITE US TOGETHER
LIKE A QUILT,
SO I WILL ALWAYS SPEAK MY
LANGUAGES WITHOUT GUILT.
I WILL NEVER BE ASHAMED TO SPEAK,
IN THIS LANGUAGE THAT IS SO UNIQUE.
BAHEBEK, MAMA.
BAHEBAK, BABA.

Glossary of Arabic Words
(Egyptian Dialect)

Habibti: My love - حبيبتي

Teita: Grandma - تيته

Shukran: Thank you - شكراً

Bahebek: I love you (feminine) - بحبِك

Bahebak: I love you (masculine) - بحبَك

Mama: Mom - ماما

Baba: Dad - بابا

Shurbet 'ads: Lentil soup - شوربة العدس

Kofta: Spiced meatball - كفته

Other English words derived from Arabic: zero, algebra, sofa, candy, alcohol, cotton

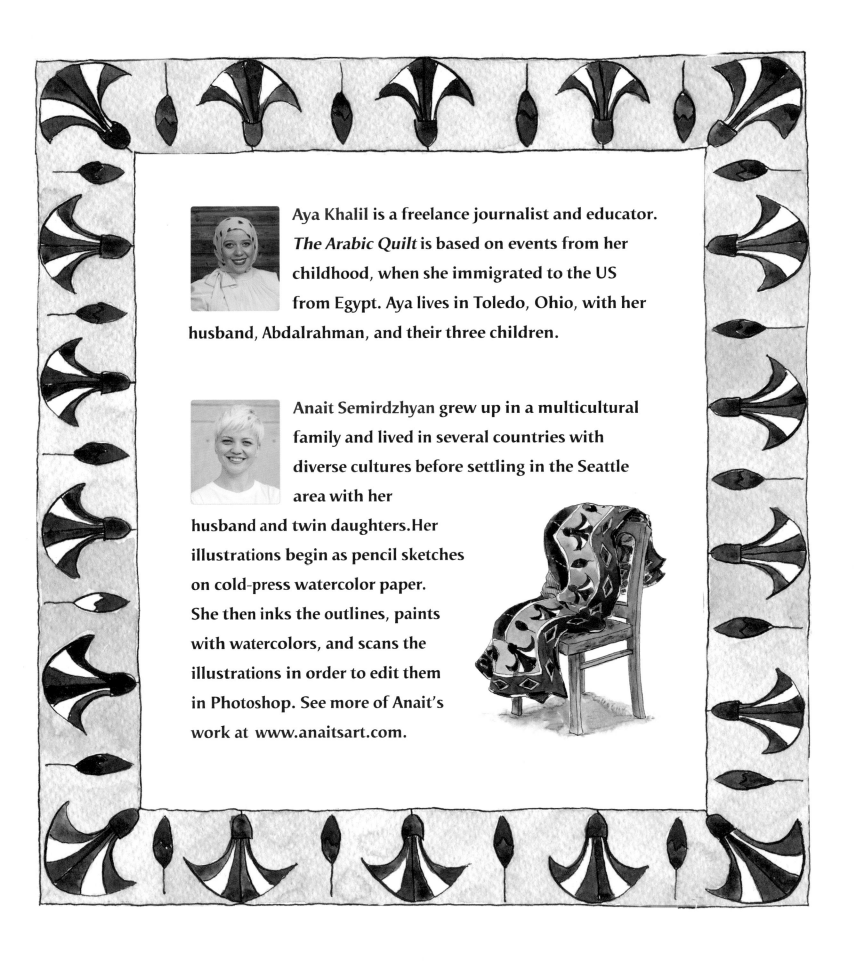

Aya Khalil is a freelance journalist and educator. *The Arabic Quilt* is based on events from her childhood, when she immigrated to the US from Egypt. Aya lives in Toledo, Ohio, with her husband, Abdalrahman, and their three children.

Anait Semirdzhyan grew up in a multicultural family and lived in several countries with diverse cultures before settling in the Seattle area with her husband and twin daughters. Her illustrations begin as pencil sketches on cold-press watercolor paper. She then inks the outlines, paints with watercolors, and scans the illustrations in order to edit them in Photoshop. See more of Anait's work at www.anaitsart.com.